D1323655

A PRINCESS
NAMED
SASMACHA

A PRINCESS NAMED SASMACHA

First Collection of Short Stories

CEDRICK MAYHEM

Rev. date: 11/21/2017

To order additional copies of this book, contact:
Xlibris
1-888-795-4274
·www.Xlibris.com
Orders@Xlibris.com
603600

A Princess Named Sasmacha

Their once was a princess named Sasmacha. Her name meant "impenetrable." She lived in the city of Wisdom, in the state of Hope, on planet Mundo.

Her husband was a powerful diplomat who traveled far and wide. He had three hundred concubines, but only one wife. His name was Fiord. His name meant "unbending." They had three daughters, also princesses. The oldest one was Belleza Hambuguesa, whose name meant "beautiful hamburger." The middle child was called Francesca Allegria, meaning "happy Frances." The baby child was named Sophia Melodia, meaning "song of Sophia."

Sasmacha lived in a mountainous region surrounded by powerful serpents. Tackhead was the largest one. He lived in the sea. He was fluorescent green with scales. His eyes were as red as fire. He was to guard the princesses for eternity.

The second one was smaller. His name was Nitro. His color was turquoise. His wingspan was seven feet. One wing was covered with one hundred eyes. The other wing had one big telescopic lens capable of a zoom view of two feet in front of your face. He constantly flew over Mundo, and his cry was like a woman giving birth. He attacked no one but reported all activity to Gaza, the land serpent.

The land serpent was a one-hundred-foot sandworm. It would go in and out beneath Mundo. He threaded his way in and out, and he was capable of emitting sticky threads that captured intruders and squeezed the life force out of their bodies within seconds.

Every inhabitant of planet Mundo emitted a scent. The scent was registered with the three serpents. One or all the three serpents would immediately detect any intruder. So life was peaceful on Mundo.

The prince was rich and powerful. Above all, he was respected in all parts of Mundo. His rule was not oppressive. Even though his name meant "unbending," he was well-thought-of and considered fair.

He had one enemy. His enemy dwelled in the center of Mundo. He chose life underground. His name was Mitar, which meant "can't wait." Mitar was of an ancient race that had almost been completely destroyed by a war. He had been the only survivor and had been promised to wed the firstborn daughter of Landor. Landor's name ("all is mine") told all. He was Sasmacha's father. On the day of the wedding, a voice from the sky boomed out and vibrated the ground and sea. It said, "There must never be intermarriage between the races of Mitar and Sasmacha." Mitar's race had been destroyed because of appetites that were forbidden.

Mitar was living proof of the power of **Dad**. **Dad** was the invisible being who caused all to become. His name meant "tender lover of all." Mitar was spared only because he was the progeny of an unnamed source that had been obliterated from the roles when the destruction came to pass. Only **Dad** knew the reason he could never marry. He was to remain celibate. He was not to give in to his sexuality, or he would lose his power. His hair would fall out. His teeth would rot. His skin would be covered with lesions.

On the day of the wedding, all of Mundo became aware of the races. Mitar had taken the news badly. His nostrils flared. His eyes bugged out, and his mouth uttered curse after curse. He started to foam at the mouth, frothy foam. It spurted from his mouth with each evil curse. He started to spin. He spun his body like a tornado. He began to tunnel underground.

Mitar had disappeared into the ground, and he was still there. His diet had changed, and it was said that he had focused all his anger completely on Fiord. He had vowed revenge, and the serpents were not allowed to interfere.

Now let's go back to the princess Sasmacha.

She lived in the north tower of the palace. Her room was decorated in scarlet, black, and gold. She had a walled garden all to herself. In it she had every variety of flowers. She had every variety of birds. She knew them all by name.

But she was sooooooooo lonely. She was lonely because her husband was so busy ruling Mundo, and with his three hundred concubines, it seemed like she did not even have a husband.

Sasmacha was not allowed to have concubines because she was female. This princess's life was filled with beauty and precious things from **Dad**. But inside, a hunger was growing in her heart. She loved **Dad** and Fiord, but she was too much a woman to endure these long absences with only the company of her children and the servants. Due to the stress of ruling Mundo, her husband had lost delight in her. She had once known that her value could not be measured. But with every year and each child, his ability to laugh and rejoice diminished little by little until the moments spent together were like some play with unlimited performances.

One day, while walking through the perfumed garden, she sat on a stone, and she began weeping. She wept tears of frustration. She wept tears of anger. Her anger was directed at **Dad** and Fiord. She sobbed; she screamed. She wailed, for when the princess Sasmacha did anything, she did it to completion. Her tears rolled down her cheek and formed a pool at her feet. Then the pool began to run like a brook, and her tears mixed with the ground of Mundo.

At that moment, a red bird, a male cardinal—the biggest, reddest cardinal she had ever seen—came to her feet. The bird put his beak into the stream of her tears and drank deeply. Were her eyes deceiving her? As he drank, he grew. His wings changed into two arms with hands. His bird feet became two legs and the feet of a man, size ten and one half. His feathers disappeared. His hair was long, black, and curly. His eyes were the warmest brown. His cheekbones were very pronounced, and when she beheld a complete man standing before her, she instantly fell in love. Her tears were magic, and her unspoken dreams and longings were transfused in the tears. The cardinal, by filling himself with her tears, became the object of her desire.

She stood still. She let her eyes drink deep the beauty she beheld. She could not move. She felt so hot. She was so weak she thought she would faint. The birdman, who she named Sanction (which means "I believe"), took a step forward and enfolded her in his arms. Without a word, he drank her lips in the same manner he had drunk her tears. He drank long and deeply. A song began in the princess, a song that was the most joyous to know; it bubbled and frothed. In the next moment, she broke free. She ran from flower to flower, singing this new song. The flowers bloomed in that instant, before their time. The sky became a bright laser-enchanted sky. She danced back and forth, running, running to and running from. The birdman looked on and formed a longing to become for this princess all she would ever need or want. A plan was formulated in his mind.

In his heart and in his eyes, he knew he could not possess her, for her name was "impenetrable." He knew that he would never be forced to leave her side or ignore her dreams and desires. He knew he was loved. He knew her love was magic. Had anyone known a healing love like this? At that time, they joined hands and frolicked in the garden. Sanction and Sasmacha played hide-and-seek. Fiord was away, and no servants were allowed in her garden. So they quite enjoyed themselves.

They barely spoke to each other, but their eyes spoke volumes. He caught her several times, and every time he caught her, he kissed her. He seemed to have fifty thousand kinds of kisses. Some were so possessive and intense she felt he would steal her tongue and never return it. His arms embraced her firmly like he had no intention of ever letting go. His hands caressed her with the tenderness of soft cotton clouds that floated over the entirety of her body. Never did he violate her sacred treasure; that was only for Fiord. Mundo had strict and precise rules for anyone who violated their marriage vows. Although Sasmacha lost her fear of death a time or two, Sanction never lost his.

They were of **Dad**. They were obedient creatures. They were innocent, blameless. And they were alive and living. This activity went on for several days. It was so new. This happiness gave her eyes a new perspective on everything. Food tasted incredible. Her daughters were enchanting. She enjoyed everything in her life. Each day was greater than the last.

***

News reached her that Fiord was returning. She had to think of what to do with her Sanction. She went to the pool of tears. She filled a bottle, and she brought it to him and said, "My dear Sanction, you must drink this and become a cardinal once more. You will live in my bedroom, in a beautiful cage, with the best diet. I will sing to you each night. You must not give attention to Fiord when he enters my bed. You must be a bird. The moment Fiord goes away, I will bring the magic tears, and you must drink and become Sanction. Then we will resume our play, our joy, and our life."

Never had anyone divorced his mate on Mundo. **Dad** had forbidden it. No one dared defile their marriage beds. Sasmacha never understood how **Dad** gave the man so much freedom to have concubines. She secretly thought that some things were not exactly fair. But she always obeyed regardless.

Sanction did not like to be in a cage. Sasmacha was so afraid of the possibility of him flying far away from her or, worse yet, of him developing nesting instincts with his own species. Even though Sanction thought it was completely against his own nature, he submitted to her will. They were very happy.

One night, in the middle of the night, after drinking much negus (which was a wine punch that the prince loved), Fiord started singing a raunchy song of how he missed the kisses of his one true love, the princess Sasmacha. He made his way up the spiral staircase. Singing and tripping, he was at her door.

"Sasmacha, Sasmacha, I want to see your beauty unfold. Allow me to enter." Sasmacha had to open the door. At once, the prince threw her down and opened her petals and satisfied himself in the manner he was accustomed to. All at once, Sanction flapped his wings in a furor. He made a cawing noise that disrupted the prince's activity.

"What's this?" exclaimed Fiord. "A new pet? How curious, my dear Sasmacha. What a racket he makes! Whatever possessed you to take such a wild bird and make him your captive pet?"

"My lord, I met him in the garden, and he was weak. I made him strong. I like his beauty. He makes me happy, my lord."

"Well, if that cawing magpie of a bird makes you happy, so be it. But cover him please, so I may complete my lust for you in peace."

"Yes, my lord. At once, my lord." Sadly she got her silk shawl and covered the cage and whispered, "Hush, my pet, he leaves tomorrow." At this news, Sanction realized he could do her no good by his fits, and he became calm.

***

The next morning, the prince set out for the region of Rusk. Fiord had to check the cherry crops. The season was upon them. The farmers loved to have him inspect their hard labor of love; cherries were the main crop of Mundo.

He left before daybreak. The rain was pouring. Sasmacha awoke at once and got her bottle of tears. "Awake, my love. Drink deep and long." The bird put his beak to the bottle and drank. Slowly, he became Sanction. Her love was reawakened, and her desires magnified. "Lie on the bed next to me, for the day is cold and dreary. I want to feel your warmth." Sanction took her into his arms and rocked gently back and forth.

He was so soothing and so comforting. Never had she known such peace. Her legs were intertwined with his. His fingers were entangled in her hair. His sounds were the cooing songs that doves make when they cry.

She was lost in a dream world, a world where she was not a princess. She was not a mother. She was just a person who was deeply loved and desired. This feeling began a crescendo in her heart, then a mezzo forte. Again, waves of ecstasy washed her body free of anxiety. She cried out, "Oh my Sanction, my eternal beloved, my *unico* perfection, my oneness, I vow to love you to my grave." She sobbed. She was happy. Her joy was unmatched in the kingdom, but she was not violated. She was Sasmacha. She was impenetrable. She was a fortress.

Sanction was also full of joy. Out of his cage, with his manly legs and torso, he strutted across the room, preening in the mirror. He flexed his muscles. He peered into his own face. He looked into his soul. He liked being a man. But it was very different. He had power. He looked at Sasmacha, her face angelic in sleep. He was at peace with himself and with **Dad**. He felt good knowing that he was responsible for her happiness—not Fiord, not her children. *Only him.*

He flapped his arms and began to sing. His song was low, and his song had no words that one could understand. They were from his bird life. But if we were to understand the words, we would not be so quick to think ourselves higher on the food chain than birds. These were words of freedom, of soaring high in the heavens. No restraint but the winds, looking down on all life, feeling confidence and excitement.

This song awoke Sasmacha. She looked at her love standing naked in front of the mirror, flapping and singing. She said, "Come to me at once again, my Sanction. I want to hold you until that moment before Fiord enters the kingdom. All else must wait. Teach me this song, my love. Tell me its meaning. Give me love, give me breath, give me life."

Sanction was the most unselfish lover. He was a tireless lover. Even though the act of love was forbidden, he was endless with affection. His kisses were like the beating of her heart. They did not stop. His touches were like massages with velvet silk and satin. He never lost control, and she began to love him ever so deeply. Part of her was ready to die for him. Only his self-control saved her from begging to die. He also wanted to live forever. He wanted her to live forever.

There were knocks on the door, but she said, "Go away. The rain has taken me to bed. You girls must entertain yourselves until your father comes home. You may just this once go to my garden and select each of you a bouquet of your favorite flowers. Just please stay away from the salt pool in the center of the garden."

Francesca, Sophia, and Belleza were delighted, for they were hardly ever allowed in her garden. They ran! It was the most beautiful place in the kingdom. They had no trouble selecting and arranging their selections. Then they went to the main hall where a feast of cherries jubilee and cherry cheesecake and cherries soufflé were waiting for them. Fiord had sent ahead of him all the choicest fruit, and he wanted all his favorite dishes prepared for his return the next day. Traveling with him was his treasurer, who made sure all his subjects were paid well for their crops. He had twenty concubines of his latest supply.

***

There were no armies in Mundo due to the scent registration. So the people lived without fear. You see, even Mitar feared **Dad**. He would never actually kill Fiord. But he could lock him up a bit for old times' sake.

From the marriage of Mitar's parents (maybe they were not really married), there was a shortage of brainpower in the center of his skull. He could never quite get his plans organized. His traps were infantile. His schemes were hokey. His ideas were full of holes. He needed someone smarter than himself to formulate a plan. As dumb as he was, he was smart enough to realize this particular fact. But who? Who indeed. Being banished to the underground hadn't really been too good for his networking skills. But Gaza, the land serpent, was a somewhat sympathetic listener. Because they frequented the same vicinity, Gaza had heard his ungodly screams in the night when he would be tormented by his cravings for the sensual pleasure with Sasmacha. She was to be his bride. Instead he was cursed to a life with no mate. Never! Ever! For eternity! It was more than he could bear.

So he asked, "Why is it that Fiord has everything? He has Sasmacha. He has the princesses. He lives in a palace. He is loved and respected by all of Mundo. I am cursed and despised for the sins of my race. It is so unfair. It is torturous for me. I am tormented by demons nightly. I am filled with twisted desires that even I do not understand. I did not create myself. I did not make myself in this fashion. Why am I so lowly? Why? Why? Why?"

Gaza was slithering by when he heard this diatribe going on. Gaza was moved to pity. He engaged him in heartfelt conversation. "Oh great and sad Mitar, what brings on this sadness? Is it the anniversary of your **Dad**-imposed vanquishing? Tell me, Mitar. This is not the first time I have encountered you like this. I would like to understand why a man would choose this life underground."

"Gaza, my friend Gaza, I had no idea there existed a sympathetic listener for the likes of me. Gaza, I am a man, but because of the sins of my race, I am punished, unbearably so. I was at the altar to wed the beautiful Sasmacha, and the voice boomed out saying **Dad** forbids the match. Then, to top it off, as if that in itself was not bad enough, I was told I must never give in to my sexuality, or I will lose my power. My hair will fall out, my teeth will rot, and my skin will be covered in lesions. All my days and all my nights are filled with lusty desires, desires that are forbidden.

"I spin, I tunnel, I cry, I plead to **Dad** to know why. Why punish me for the sins of my father? I look at myself in the mirror. I know I'm not an ugly man to behold. What good is my beauty if I cannot love or be loved in the way that is natural for me? I think I'm better off dead. The thought of never getting revenge on Fiord for having what is or was to be mine is all I'm living for. Sweet revenge. Then I can go to the grave. Dark secrets lurk inside my brain, whispering madness that drives me insane. I want fulfillment. I want it all.

"But **Dad** never lies. To come to an end in such a helpless, disgusting way is more than I can bear. So I wait. But my name means 'can't wait.' Still I wait, and I wait some more. Gaza, it is kind of you to listen, but this is making me worse. I'm in a frenzy. I've been told Fiord is passing this way on the way back from Rusk. Gaza, help me, Gaza, please? I know you have been told not to interfere, but maybe some innocent aid would be appropriate at this time. I have no one. He has everything. My envy burns inside my brain. If I could, I would kill him ever so slowly. I would kidnap the princesses and rape them every night for eternity. If not for my fear of **Dad**, I would do those things. Especially Sasmacha. I would tie Fiord to a post and lie with her. I would penetrate what Fiord has stolen from me. Yes!"

Gaza replied, "You are very disgusting, Mitar, and although I do have some fellow feeling for you, I can't think that you are anything but trouble for me. I am guardian serpent of the land of Mundo. I am powerful. I could squeeze the life force out of you just for saying your ugly sayings. I grant that I will do you no harm, but I refuse to take part in your schemes. I, too, obey **Dad**.

"Do not forget, He caused us to become. Oh, I guess He did you no favor, eh, Mitar. Why don't you ask for a retrial? Ask for some answers. Ask as a son. Ask humbly and tell Him of your suffering."

"Gaza, oh, Gaza, I want to. Somehow my petitions and my words combine with my anger, and I end up sounding like a whiny old woman. But there is always tomorrow. Thank you, Gaza, and good day to you."

"Good day to you, Mitar. I will speak with you again soon."

***

Fiord was on his sixth concubine for the day, and he told his treasurer, who was sampling cherries and eating to his satisfaction, "Let us continue our journey home. I have a sudden craving for the princess Sasmacha. It is funny, but these concubines are falling short these days. Do you think I might need new ones?"

"Well, my lord, three hundred is a large number, and these twenty are of your newest acquisitions. No, my lord. It is just that Sasmacha is your wife, your impenetrable possession that you share with no one. You have married her at a great cost. She was to be married to Mitar, and you have stolen her from her destiny—or rescued her, as the people say in Mundo. She is quite a prize. It is only natural for you to desire her company, my lord. Why do you feel strongly about it?"

"Well, I guess it's because I haven't been feeling that way for the longest time, and now that I do, it is foreign to me."

"Do you not love your wife, sire? Surely you do."

"Yes, of course, I love her, but what does love have to do with lust?"

"Ah ha! Oh yes, my lord, I understand now. Well, then, we must hurry on our way home. Come one, come all into the chariots. Away we go to Wisdom. It won't be long now, and your princess will be in your arms once more."

"Thank you, Gene. Now send number seven back to me and shut the curtain and go back to your cherries. Enough of this talking. Away with you!"

"Yes, my lord."

***

Back at the palace, the three princesses were in the kitchen with the cook making grand soufflés, along with huge cheesecakes and cherries jubilees, like no one had ever seen. They loved their father. He was handsome and generous and kind to them. He always brought them presents.

Francesca had asked for a magic watch. She was told that the watch could be set backward in time or forward three times. You would experience that twenty-four-hour period either in the past or in the future.

Sophia had asked for a pink lamb that could sing fifty songs. She loved animals and music. She was a kind and gentle child.

Belleza had asked for one hundred hamburgers to have a party for some of her friends. She loved to dance and eat and talk to boys. She was the lively one.

They were all good girls. They delighted their parents, and the parents were enchanted with the children. It was a happy day.

Sasmacha had been in bed the whole time. She opened the windows and let the fresh air in. She ran to her garden for her bottle of tears. She came back, and she saw Sanction looking in the mirror, looking happy. She felt happy and sad. Sanction had delighted her with his stories, his poetry, his songs, and his touches. She said to him, "My love, my life, it's time to drink again. I am yours forever, I'll always be yours."

Sanction replied, "Your happiness is mine, and I am yours forever. You are my only love. These days with you are the most wonderful I've known. I like being your man, but sometimes I miss my bird life. In the day, dear princess, may I be free to fly in the garden and in your room?"

"Sanction, my dear Sanction, what you ask, you will be given. But only promise not to fly away from me. Promise that, and I will grant you your wish."

"I promise."

"OK, now drink and become my beautiful red bird because the chariot has arrived."

"Yes, my lady." Sanction drank and became smaller and smaller. His feathers were such a bright red. There was no more black silky hair. He was the most beautiful bird. Also, he was the most beautiful man. She loved him both ways.

"Back to your cage. My husband is approaching quickly."

No sooner was Sanction back in his cage than Fiord burst into the room.

"What's this? Princess, you were not expecting me? You are not bathed and prepared, and your room is a mess. Are you ill? What is the matter? Tell me at once."

"Well, my lord, you see, it's the rain. Yes, it's the rain. The rain made me melancholy and blue. I've been all alone, singing the blues, because I've missed you so much, my love," she lied.

"Oh, my chickadee, then I believe we are on the same wavelength. Come to me, Sasmacha. Give me what is mine, all mine. Open your petals and receive your husband and your prince. Receive me with rejoicing, for I have a great need for you."

***

"Ahhhhhhhhhhhh! That was good! Was that not the greatest love for you, my pet?"

"Oh yes, my lord," she lied quickly.

Fiord was so elated. She was a good wife. He loved his wife.

But Sanction was upset. How dare this man treat this woman like a whore! Why didn't she tell him? Why didn't she tell him "no, my lord, you were not great. I did not have time to blink my eye"? Sanction started flapping.

"In the name of **Dad**, what's this commotion?"

"It's nothing, my lord, it's my pet. I forgot to cover him."

"I see, still nurturing the wild bird. Why don't you let him go? He probably wants a mate. It's unnatural for him to be caged. I'd be flapping too if you did that to me."

"No, my lord, do not say those things. He likes his cage. He is protective of me. He thinks you are hurting me."

"Well, be quick and cover him up. I want some more of you before I go to bed. Come now and be a good girl. That's right, Sasmacha, come to papa."

She had no choice but to cover Sanction with her silk shawl and reassure him that in two more days Fiord would be gone.

Sanction, as a bird, was helpless in his cage. He had visions of pecking Fiord's eyes so he would be blind. He would then play hide-and-seek. Only, he would hide Sasmacha, and Fiord would blindly seek. Oh, what a vision! But if he encountered him when he was in his man form, he would challenge him to a duel. Winner takes all—the castle and all that came with it. With these visions, he was able to sleep. Fiord was sated.

Only Sasmacha was awake. She was confused. How could she be living separate lives in one body? She did love her husband. She adored her children. But this love for Sanction, the birdman, was so different, so unnameable, so celestial and satisfying, not to mention magnificent. Where would it all end? But how could one think of ending it when it had all just begun? *Let me dream of flying. I'm no widow*, she thought. *I'm no spinster. My womb has been blessed. My breasts have been suckled. I am the happiest woman in the kingdom. There exists no one fuller than I.* On that merry note, she fell into a deep sleep.

***

The next two days passed quickly, and Fiord was on his way to Magi, the little province by the sea. He was to give a speech on the blessings received from **Dad** this year, to give thanks for the bounteous crops. He took with him his spiritual advisor and ten concubines. On the way, he consulted Gaza, Nitro, and Tackhead to make sure there would be no disturbances. So everything would remain calm on Mundo. Gaza almost revealed the distress of Mitar, but he withdrew from the conversation and decided to keep a good eye on him himself. So they set off.

***

Speaking of Mitar. Mitar had spent another torturous night. He desperately wanted to die. Mitar was raging against Fiord. He was planning out a deceptive plan to kidnap and torture him endlessly. He knew he could not rely on Gaza. Somehow, some way, but how?

Let's see. I think a plan is formulating. He would get the hoodoo man to conjure up a scent like no one on Mundo—an evil scent. Then he would gather all the serpents to capture the intruder. When all the serpents were busy, he would give the concubines and the advisor knockout drops and nab the prince. Yes! Yes! Yes! That was what he would do. Excellent plan! He knew one of the concubines; her name was So So, meaning "I don't care." He would get her to help him deceive Fiord. *Ha ha, the plot thickens.*

He set off to visit So So. She lived in Canyon Park, on the other side of Grapevine. She was a sensual, luscious babe. She had two little wings on her shoulder blades. When she became sexually excited, she beat her wings until she fell out and had to be revived. That's why she appealed to Fiord. So Mitar, the sexless suffragette, set off.

He arrived at the precise moment she had come from Magi. Fiord had used her for two days of the journey, so she was ready for some real action. Mitar knocked at her door. She answered in a squeaky voice, "Yes, now what?"

"It is I, Mitar. I beg to see you."

"Open the door, Mitar. I am here reclining."

"Hello, So So. My, but you are a sight for sore eyes. If only you, my pet, could be my bride."

"Well, Mitar, why do you choose that wretched life underground with no mate, no love, and no food?"

"So So, it is **Dad**. It is His wish for me, and I must obey."

"Mitar, I could make you sooooo happy!"

"Yes, So So, but then the curse. You know it won't happen to you. It will happen to me."

"Oh, Mitar, everyone knows that the curse is just a joke. It's silly. It would never happen in a million years."

"What's this you say? So So, you do not believe the curse to be true?"

"Of course not, it's **Dad**'s joke on us. *Haha!* Oh, Mitar, all this time you thought all those horrible things would happen to you? Mitar, I'll be your wife. Let's get started."

So So's wings started to beat. *Wow! Could this be true?* First, he must convince So So to help him with Fiord.

"So So, this has taken me aback. Could you please promise me something? I will marry you if you help me avenge my race's blood. I want you to give Fiord these drops in his wine. Then, my precious, you must allow me to enter. I will kidnap Fiord. I will torture him until he agrees to grant me a kingdom of my own to rule. Then, my luscious babe, you will be my queen. Do you agree?"

"Yes, Mitar. Yes, my husband. Yes, my king."

"Then let's seal our fate with a kiss. This is ancient Baca fashion." Baca is Mitar's race. *Baca* means "back off." So So lay on the floor. Mitar put his lips over hers without their bodies touching. Mitar's legs were facing south while he was lying on his stomach. Then he progressed down her body. Her words were stuttering. Would he? Could he? Should he? These were the questions raging in his mind. Well, Mitar's last thoughts before he sank into her sensual softness were **Dad**, **Dad**, *forgive me,* **Dad**.

***

Fiord was on concubine number eight and was ready to go home. He was tired. Nobody knew the responsibilities he had. It was overwhelming. He ruled all of Mundo. That's a lot of ruling!

Sasmacha didn't understand the pressure. She was always lighthearted and protected. She was always ready for frolicking. But Fiord? Fiord worried too much. The concubines just relieved the pressure, that's all. Sasmacha was his true love. Then he had a thought. What if Sasmacha had concubines? What if Sasmacha relieved her pressure, be it so small? What if? Big thought.

His Sasmacha spreading her petals for other men? Stronger men? Prettier men? Men who smelled better? Holy moly! Santa caracollas! He'd never thought of that. That's disgusting! Well, she'd never! She wouldn't, she couldn't, she definitely shouldn't.

Did it bother her that he had concubines? It's quite possible that if it bothered him, it just might bother her. Oh, how stupid he had been all this time! He must change. He must get rid of them at once. He must tell her at once. But on that thought, the beautiful So So sashayed into the room.

He blurted out, "Not now, not now. I must send you away tonight. I set you free. As of now, you are no longer my concubine. Go away!"

"Oh wait, my lord. Please do not be so quick in this new decision. I've been quite good for you, no? I think you must agree to one eensy, weensy, teensy drinky poo. Puleeeeeese?"

"Oh, So So, sure, why not? I owe you that. Take some cherries for yourself. Here is a piece of land to call your own. It is called Pagan Place. You will be fine. You will be great. Ummmmmmm, good wine. Uuummmmmmmmmmm, good night."

And so Fiord was out like a light. So So was sipping champagne, waiting for Mitar. Mitar entered. He rolled Fiord up in the carpet, and he and So So lugged it to the underland rover outside. No one knew. No one saw. It was perfect, no? Then Mitar told So So to stay and act drugged too and to not know a thing.

So she played dead until discovered.

***

Sasmacha was sailing in her moat with Sanction. She had had a wonderful day. Sanction gave her piggyback rides all through the garden. She loved all that bouncing. She had no inkling of what was to happen.

On the day the news arrived, she gave Sanction the magic tears, and he was already a red bird. The entourage arrived, but no Fiord. No one dared to gossip about it. The news was brought to the princess first. She was astounded. She questioned the three serpents individually and collectively. She could not believe such a thing could and did happen. Her heart was afraid for Fiord. She wanted answers to questions. She wanted them now. She wanted them yesterday.

The serpents were put on total surveillance of the planet Mundo. They were to get the people to help them find Fiord. Meanwhile, she gathered the princesses. She let them know that a bad thing had come to pass in their lives. They must pull together as a family to help their father, and they must not let the kingdom run rampant. She must take control and rule and control the populace. Big job!

In the meantime, no one was to know about the disappearance. It was the guarded secret of the castle. The serpents were to question all of Mundo. It was to be systematically accomplished. Door to door. House to house. The king must be found.

***

Back in the woods, Mitar had gagged Fiord and put him in the trunk of the underland rover. No concubines now. Only silence, darkness, immobility. Fiord was a king. He was a mighty king. He was not easily scared. Right now, he was unconscious—unaware of where he was and whom he was with. He was just along for the ride so far. But Mitar was ahead of the party. He was preparing a place for Fiord underground—a place of darkness and unending physical agony. No peace, no goodness, no light. In other words, *jail*. Jail was the ultimate fate of the unrighteous, and there he was going to be.

***

Back at the castle, Sasmacha was formulating her own plan. She did not want the kingdom to know the reason for the door-to-door search. So she put out a bulletin that read:

"Lost! The biggest, brightest, most perfect ——."

The last word was unreadable. Everyone was asked to find the biggest, brightest, most perfect ——. They were searching everywhere, even though they were not clear on what it was they were searching for.

The serpents were not allowed to interfere in this instance. They were not to use their power. This was strictly between Mitar and Fiord. The heat was on.

***

Fiord regained consciousness. He was in the darkness. The blackest black. No light. No gray. Nothing but black. He had had no idea how much the light meant to him. He was awed. He was ashamed of how little regard he had for the light until it was gone. There was nothing but black. It was a nightmare. Jail was the absolute worst situation in all of Mundo. Nothing compared. The ultimate torture! It was insanity. How much black can you see? He didn't even know it was Mitar who put him in the darkness. He was really in the dark.

It was said in the beginning that Mitar's brainpower was not capable of a perfect plan. Mitar had gone to the hoodoo man. He had asked for the scent, the evil scent. The serpents were already tracking it. Mitar had talked to Gaza about his hatred of Fiord. He had gone to the hoodoo man with his request.

These two were loyal subjects of Fiord's with no loyalty to Mitar. They also loved the princess Sasmacha, and they were devoted to the three young princesses. They immediately went to the princess with their information. They put two and two together, and it all added up to Mitar. Although the serpents were not allowed to interfere, they were not forced to keep silent about what was going down. All they saw and heard was to be reported to her.

She and her people had to do all the work. They would succeed. It was just a matter of time. Sasmacha was distracted and distraught, but by no means was she defeated.

***

Sanction was really moved by how deeply Sasmacha loved her husband. He vowed he would not selfishly try to take advantage of this situation. He would put Sasmacha's feelings first. He would find Fiord for her. But to do that, he would be better off in his bird form. So off he flew, up in the sky, for a bird's-eye view of Mundo. *Wow!* How long had he been kept in that cage? How he had missed this. He had forgotten what it felt like to fly and soar above the world. This was indescribable. He had missed it badly.

Being a man was great, but he couldn't be a man all the time—or be with Sasmacha. Sanction made a decision. He decided to give up Sasmacha. He would find Fiord for her, and then he would disappear. He would force her to confront Fiord with her sadness and frustration. She would have no other alternative.

It would be the most difficult, unselfish act he had ever committed as a bird or a man. This is what true love is about—putting your lover's well-being first. He was truly in love with Sasmacha. With a heavy heart and with his mind made up, off he flew on the quest that would take his love out of his life . . . forever.

***

At the palace, the princess was engaged in a deep conversation with the three princesses. She knew the serpents weren't allowed to use their powers. So the princesses of Mundo were uniting to use their powers—their gifts. All of a sudden, Francesca Allegria blurted out, "Mother! I have an idea."

"What is it?" they all exclaimed.

"Mother, let's use the magic watch Father bought me. We will set it backward to the day before Papa disappeared. Then we will have the serpents pick up Mitar and bring Papa back before he was kidnapped."

"Wonderful little child you are! What a brilliant idea! How clever! What do you think, Sophia and Belleza?"

"Mama, I think our sister is a genius," said Belleza.

"Mama, I want Papa back. Mama, let's do it," said Sophia.

"Tonight we sleep on it. We must talk to **Dad**. We must ask Him to bless our efforts."

"Yes," said Belleza. "Let's all spend the night together. Let's all talk to **Dad** together, and tomorrow we act! By this time tomorrow, if all succeeds, we will have our prince and our father home."

***

Nitro was flying surveillance. His eyes were everywhere. Tackhead was in the sea. He was underwater. He swam to the bottom, looking for anything suspicious. He went to the top of the water, stirring it up. He was angry that this had happened to the prince right under his scales. Gaza was in and out of the earth. He hadn't seen Mitar since the last encounter. That worried him. All they could do was wait for Mitar's stupidity to manifest itself, and it would.

***

Mitar and So So were romping in the hay every chance they got. He was a lost soul, and he was love starved. Her wings were beating, and she was falling out five times a day. They didn't even check on Fiord. They just tossed his food in the *jail*.

It would hit him on the head. He would cry out, "Who is there? Get me out of here!" But all he would hear was laughter. *Ah ha ha ha!* Masculine and feminine laughter, then nothing. Just darkness. He would bend down and feel the floor. There would be some old black cherries with the pits. There would be some hard bread and rank cheese.

He had to eat it. He had to live. He had so much to live for. He had to live to see Sasmacha and the princesses. He had to live to tell how wrong he had been all this time and what he had learned about concubines. So he ate and he ate and he did not grow weak. He remained strong. He had faith in his serpents, in **Dad**. He had faith that sustained him. He had faith in his subjects.

***

At the palace, the princesses were ready to set the watch. It was set to the day before the disappearance—August 27, 2000.

They had spent the night in Fiord's bed together, talking to **Dad**. They felt it was the best course to take.

A push of the button on the watch, and Fiord was just finishing his revelation about concubines. The serpents picked up his scent. Nitro and Gaza immediately traced Fiord. They escorted him back to the palace.

Sanction was not affected by the magic watch as he was in his bird form. It didn't affect animals.

Mitar and So So were apprehended and brought to the palace. You see, although they didn't recall what had happened, it was all documented so the proper action could be taken. The door-to-door search was halted. The people were gathered. All were in expectation of the outcome of this fantastic plot.

The sky opened, and what looked like a throne came down from the sky. The brightest light was emitted from the throne. A voice boomed, "Mitar, come forward!"

Mitar was afraid. Mitar was sick of being the villain, the scapegoat for evil. He had decided to take Gaza's advice. He approached the throne, and these were his words:

"Dear **Dad**, I humbly approach Your magnificent light. Have mercy on me. I am so wretched. Please forgive the sins of my race. I alone survived by Your mercy. **Dad**, death is more welcome than this life. I know I am in line to receive Your curse. I know my fate is sealed. I only wanted a wife, some respect as a human. **Dad**, Your will be done, not mine. If You pardon me, I will obey You and cause You no pain, no regrets for forgiving me. I never laid a hand on Fiord. I just showed him the dark side of life. It is the worst fate of man. I will serve You. I will be a loyal subject. Please take away the curse. How long must a soul pay for the mistakes of his father?"

"Silence! Mitar, I have read your heart. Your revenge on Fiord has been your driving force. I do have mercy on you. I have listened to your pleas. From this day forward, I remove the curse. I forgive your race. I grant So So to become your bride. I grant one-quarter of the kingdom to be yours to rule. Today there is a truth to be revealed.

"You see, I was alone in the heavens. I yearned for a companion. I yearned for a helper, a son. Not to equal me or eclipse me, but to stay by my side. I made your father. I formed him from the elements of Mundo. I breathed life into his nostrils. He came to be a living soul. He had all of Mundo. That wasn't enough. He wanted more. He wanted to be me. He plotted. I let him go about his foul ways for an appointed time.

"Then, when all of Mundo was diseased, rotten, corrupted, smelling, I stepped in. I destroyed all of Mundo. Every living, breathing thing. You were the only survivor. I arranged for you to propagate the whole planet. I couldn't take the chance of ever having to destroy in that capacity again. So I changed my plan. I kept you frozen inside of Mount Victory for a set amount of time. I created another being—Landor, Sasmacha's father. Landor was like me in all my qualities—the kindness, gentleness, and tender loving.

"Yet he was a fair ruler. He has proved faithful and true. Mitar, your father's name was erased from the roles, never to exist again. But you, Mitar, were spared. Not for a mockery. For an example of the power of forgiveness and compassion. Your torment was to end when—and only when—you learned to humble yourself and ask for forgiveness.

"Now I confess a sacred secret. I am Fiord's father. Fiord has been infused with dynamic energy. He has no fleshly mother or father. He is my direct progeny, and all must obey. That is why his rule is perfect, not oppressive. You two will be brothers from now on.

"And to all the people of Mundo who were faithful and true, who went knocking door to door, searching for the biggest, brightest, most perfect ———. I grant you the reward!"

"But, **Dad**? What is the last word?"

"Yes, what do we get?"

"Yes, the biggest, brightest, most perfect what?"

"It is life. The biggest, brightest, most perfect life without end."

And all of Mundo went rejoicing—rejoicing and blessing **Dad**. Mitar and Fiord and Sasmacha and her princesses, along with the serpents and the people, prepared for the feast of all time. All their dishes were prepared to eat. They had much negus to drink. Everyone danced.

Nitro fixed each eye with lights and flew over Mundo proclaiming the glory of **Dad**.

Gaza gave all the people and the children rides on his back all over Mundo.

Tackhead turned the sea into a magic circus where all the sea animals gave rides and performed.

The three princesses were exalted for their beauty, their brains, and their loyalty. They were each given their own castle.

Belleza was given an unlimited supply of hamburgers, parties, and boys to dance with.

Francesca was given the position of keeper of time. Anytime she wanted, she could set her watch back to this happy day in their lives and relive it and then return to the present life.

Sophia was put in charge of all the animals. She was their leader. They all knew her voice and followed her, and she sang to them. She knew more songs than anyone on Mundo.

Fiord gave Sasmacha gold rings—one for each finger and toe. He vowed before all of Mundo that there would never be any more concubines. One wife or forever remain celibate.

Sasmacha was so happy and busy she never even missed her birdman. The tear pool has long since dried up. They all lived in their own castles and got together frequently with great rejoicing. The joy and happiness of all of Mundo has become a legend. In fact, if you ever go to the nearest travel agency, I suggest you book a trip to Mundo in advance. It is never out of season.

THE END

The Legend of Sissy Sprout

OK, confession time. My first night in Soloman's house, it was dirty, uninhabited, and smelled like mildew. Twenty years of my life were in boxes. I was mourning the death of a marriage that somehow, I couldn't bring myself to end. It was also the end of a four-year love affair that was over after the first six months. I was a diamond peg in a square hole. Anyway, self-belief was way low, while Abba belief was way high.

I had no money and no job, so I was faced with total self-reliance. Right? What a concept for this one who had made a living out of batting eyes and oohing and ahhing over men's muscles and playing the helpless female. Why? As a con? Hell no! It was because the women of the fifties drilled it into my head.

Well, I refused to cry one more damn tear over a worthless wonder that called himself a man. I breathed. There was no heat and no electricity! Except I did have my own energy. I had sun power, moon power, and star power (not to mention star quality). I had cardboard power. Boxes! I breathed in what I did have. I exhaled what I didn't have, deeming it unnecessary, almost unwanted. I began to see myself as privileged.

God, look at all these fools with man's things. Candlelight is divine; no woman is ugly in candlelight. So no pity party for me. Hell, this time last year, I was a cripple, with no use of my right arm.

I had no car, and I walked eight blocks to the bus stop to catch a bus to go to a job that paid $7.50 an hour, only to receive a check with a 20 percent garnishment.

Yes, she had a defaulted student loan; she had borrowed the money for school when she divorced her first husband. She had a five-year-old daughter, beautiful Marcella-Donné. She had been pregnant with her second child from her immigrant student husband who had no permission to work yet.

She had made ten grand last a year and even took a trip to her husband's country, Venezuela. She hadn't wanted to return to North America. She had lost herself in the tropical beauty of the place and the love of family that existed there.

That had been in 1988. Now, twenty years later, they were asking her to pay $30,000. She had received many deferments and forbearances without understanding the principle of daily compounded interest.

So this is what I have to say to all that. Fuck the system. They can take a pound of flesh out of my ass. Put me in prison, Uncle Sam. If you really loved us, you would give us free education instead of all these war machines and outer space travel that aren't going to get you away from paying for all your rapes and murders. I owe you shit! Go suck a banana for your $30,000. Ha!

Anyway, I dream I am a servant girl, a slave girl. I've been owned by six masters, all cruel but one—the third one. My third-eye relationship is still my friend. Here they are, in alphabetical order:

B = two years
E = two years
F = four years
R = four years
L = twenty-two years
T = four years

Now, as I am a free woman, I (almost) long for those old masters. Who is going to tell me what to do, where to go, what to wear, how to wear my hair? Whose —— do I serve?

Damn, no one? That's the answer, ladies and gentlemen. I can't tell you what a freaking concept that is. Since I was born, I was serving— my god, my father, my mother, my sister, my brother, my friends, my teachers. I was a regular ass-kisser. I wanted the proverbial pat on the head. Good girl! Serve myself? What do I even want? What do I even need? What makes me happy? Big questions, little girl.

Because in all my serving, I realized that I served because I wanted to. I liked being a slave. I had experienced one good master who gave me gifts and praise and love and kindness. But that was New Orleans. Kansas City was a lot different.

Jesus served. They spit on him, hated him, lied about him, misconstrued all he did. I began to rejoice. Gandhi served; as did Mother Teresa. Hell, all great people serve. Only pompous assholes wait to be served. I wasn't waiting around to be served. I was waiting for orders, instructions, details for living on my own. I spent thirty-six years serving.

I still feel like the girl living under her father's roof, watching him fix cars and appliances and giving the neighborhood boys haircuts, chastising them and telling them to straighten up and fly right. My dad never charged the mothers or grandmas for his help.

One of the boys had married her sister. Her sister had been nine years older than her, kind of like Marcella was five years older than Marina-Delfina and Roxanne-Simone. Her mother had been married to an unspeakable man before her father had taken her and adopted her child. Was she following her mother's footsteps? Well, anyway, let me tell you this dream.

First, allow me to hit my pipe and let the herb reveal to you this sacred dream. One second. (*Inhale*) Abba, Abba, Abba (*exhale*). Shuaa aaaaaaaaaaaaaaaaaaaaaaaaaaaaaaaaaa!

OK, I am a slave girl. I have wristbands and armbands. I also have an upside-down heart tattooed on my heart. It is a prism heart. I am told the king is hungry and I am to go to the king and offer my breast to him to let him suck—to nourish and sustain him, to nurture him and heal him.

Humbly, I go to the king, for he is approachable. I do not say a word, for this is *prophesy*. I undid my blouse and looked invitingly into his eyes as I glanced down at my little breast. I timidly but happily cupped my left breast and looked up and offered it to the king.

The king stopped what he was doing and looked at me with what seemed to be amusement. "What's this?" he said in his incredible sexy, toe-curling voice that is making me squishy just typing it. It was his tone, accent, all the above.

I said, "Here they are," as I cupped the right one and smilingly offered both breasts to him. My knees were unsteady, and I felt I might swoon. I was exposed yet unashamed.

I was just too excited. Although my breasts had been suckled by many men, none of them had been of the caliber or majesty as this one who was looking like he was amazed at my audacity to even come to him and open my blouse to him.

Then, after an unbearable silence, his laughter rang out. It would have been oh so pleasant if she knew it was not directed at her personally. "You! Little girl? You think you can nourish, sustain, nurture a king, your king, on those little bitty titties? My two-year-old sister has bigger titties on her. What do you think I could possibly get from those two twin pencil erasers? Where's the tits? All I see are two rather long nipples, but no flesh. Little girl, I am a king, your king, and I have a big mouth, see?" He opened his mouth, and she grew still as she watched him open wide, wider, widest, until it looked like he could swallow her whole body easily.

"Holy shit!" She was freaking out. What kind of a god would send a little girl, a slave girl, to the king to offer her two humble small tatas for food for such a great, grand man. She wanted the floor to open and swallow her forever.

But the kind king saw that he had humiliated the bejesus out of her, changed his expression, and said, "I applaud your courage, brave one. Not many slave girls would dare to flash the king. Allow me to examine these little titties. Come forward!"

Ahhh, shit! She felt like Dorothy when she approached the wizard of Oz.

"Hmmmmmmmmmmmmmmm, here is my answer to you," the king said. "Go home and return in four weeks, on the night of the new moon. Now go!"

She buttoned her blouse and exited the throne room.

***

One of the chiefs of staff had been observing the whole affair. He liked this rather strange girl. He desired her, so he approached and said, "I overheard your conversation with the king, and I have sympathy for you. I was wondering if you would allow me to help you with your quest."

"Oh yes, my lord, anything, I'll do anything." She was an obedient child.

"Now step into my chambers for a bit of piracy—I mean, privacy." She went in willingly.

"Now open your blouse and allow me to see what we are working with," he said. "Child, what is your name?"

"My name's Sissy Sprout. May I ask yours?"

"My name is Chief Executor Mildew, but you may call me Mild."

"OK. Mild, do you think you can help me?"

Now Mild was thinking on a whole different level. He was totally over the moon and intoxicated with this girl Sissy's breasts. They were the perfect teats for him. They were not quite a handful and were deliciously a mouthful. When exposed to air, the nipples enlarged and erected so that all the brown was sticking out quite far.

Mild was salivating. *Oh my god, I've got to get this girl into the castle. I will be her tutor. Yes, she will be my protégé. I will instruct her in the ways of pleasing King Ahlowya. What a delightful task that will be.*

To the girl, he said, "Tell me, Sissy, how does it feel if I do this?"

He stuck out his hand as if to touch her breast, and she leaped three feet backward and exclaimed, "Sir, it is not for you to be touching these breasts. Even though small and humble, they are most definitely reserved for King Ahlowya. I must beg you to appreciate that fact."

This girl was full of surprises. First she barged into the throne room offering her exquisite breasts, then she had the audacity to chastise him. He had thought he had it in the bag. Now his composure was shaken. "Well, my sassy maid, I was only trying to assist you. You see, I have expertise in the art of manipulation and stimulation of women's breasts. Because of my expert techniques, the breasts actually increase in size.

So you see, if you let me, you will return to the king with astonishing results."

Hmmmmm, this sounded fishy to Sissy, but she could afford no enemies in the castle. She sweetened her reply. "Oh, that is very nice indeed. I have my mother and eight wiseass sisters who all have big breasts, so I'm sure they will have the answers to this situation. I'm just following orders."

"Yes, and by the way, whose orders might that be?"

"It came straight from **Big Daddy**. He chose me out of all my sisters, and boy, are they pissed. They won't talk to me. I know they love me. It's not my fault. You know **Big Daddy** can sometimes have a whacked-out sense of humor. Anyway, I'm not giving up. I'm sure any girl would just die for your manipulations, but I feel strongly that if I would do it, I would be defiled and my milk sour. So thanks but no thanks. I must be going now. I will be back when the time is right."

"Yes, yes, dear girl, of course. Run along now, and take good care of those titties. They really are exquisite."

***

So off Sissy went, out of the castle, through the gate, into the lane where her brother, the butcher, lived. She wondered if she should tell him. *I wonder what Mom is going to say*, she mused. Not to mention her wiseass sisters. They were going to have a field day.

She had better go straight home. She needed to meditate to get an answer from **Big Daddy**. **Big Daddy** lived in the sky, way up in a high-rise condo that only housed Him and His cronies—144,000, to be exact. Not to mention His yes-men.

She passed by the butcher shop. She went into the field and passed the meadow where there was a little brook that had seven beautiful goldfish in it. There she sat on a rock.

She began to breathe. She took long deep breaths, filling up her chest with sweet meadow air. *Shuuuuuwaa.* She exhaled rather loudly. She breathed in. *Abba, Abba, Abba.* She exhaled. *Shuwaaaaaaa.* She began to feel calm.

All at once, a goldfish poked his head out of the water. He had been watching her intently. She bent from the waist and leveled her back flat. She looked upside down backward between her legs. She locked her arms around her knees. She exhaled. *Shuwaaaaaaa*. It was then she noticed the goldfish.

"Oh, hello, who are you, Mr. Fishy?"

"I am the magnificent Neo, and I've been watching you. You are a cute girl upside down. Do you feel better?"

"Yes, Neo. In fact, I do. I've just come from seeing the king. I need to chill. I need to think about everything that was said, figure out what I must do. This is my Abba Shua meditation you caught me at. It really helps me focus."

"Oh, you dear girl, you actually saw King Ahlowya?"

"Yes, Neo, I sure did."

"Young lady, you haven't told me your name. What are you called?"

"They call me Sissy Sprout, but my friends call me Sprout. Do you want to be my friend?"

"Yes, Sprout, I really do."

"Cool, I think I will jump in and have a swim, if you don't mind. I'm in a state of physical agitation and excitement. Physical exercise is what I crave. Do you mind if I join you?"

"Certainly not, Sprout, come on in. The water's fine."

She removed her simple frock, and because she was poor, she had no underwear. She became one with the water. It was heavenly liquid, warm, enveloping, calming.

She began to swim, and she forgot about Neo, who was keeping up, jumping in and out as he swam alongside his newfound friend.

"Hey, Neo, what's that glittering down there in the center of the pool? I never noticed that before. Is it far? Can we go down there? It's so pretty. Neo, I want to get it. How far down is that?"

"Oh, Sissy, don't you know this pool is called Clear Blue Easy? You see clear down to the bottom, which makes it look easy. But! You see, everything on this planet is not as it seems to be. If you, I mean you as a human girl, were to dive in and begin to swim toward the glittering thing, you would proceed quite well until the point of no return. You see, once you realize the illusion, it would be too late to turn back, and you'd have two choices. You return for air, which is vertualy impossible, and you drown here and now. Or you evolve into a sea creature, but you maintain land status. Dig?"

"Wow, I dig, Neo! I've always wondered what it would be like to live under the sea as you do. From what I've seen, it's the best way of life. It is truly amazing. No other way can be found. Take me down, sweet Neo. You little prince of a goldfish, I'm ready!"

"Sissy, Sissy, Sissy. You *think* you are ready. In reality, you are a babe to the mature, unadulterated lifestyle that belongs to *moi*! But I, fair maiden, can take you to someone who most definitely can instruct you. His name is Smoke Fountain, not to be confused with Smoke Mountain."

"Where does Smoke Fountain live, Neo?"

"He lives in Soloman's temple. It is said that when Soloman dreams, he enters Smoke Fountain, and then the wise words of wisdom he sends out through his vibrations. They vibrate on a frequency that is so low only humans can pick up on it. So here is what you do: pick your question carefully."

"Why is that, Neo?"

"You only get one question per lunar cycle, and today is the new moon, not to be confused with the blue moon. So today it is."

"OK, I get it. Don't rush me. Well, let's see. Can this question pertain to any subject? If so, consider my question I must. I must not rush into it. You see, on one hand, I need to know how to increase my bust size so as to be able to accommodate King Ahlowya's rather large mouth, to let him feed on my breasts, which are, as we speak, so humble. On the other hand, I do indeed want to dive in the pool and get whatever is glittering out there and see what it is and what it's for and what it goes to and what it does."

"I get it, Sissy, *enough*! Well, you say your meditation is the key, yeah? So why don't you return to your meditation, and I'll watch?"

"Now I think, for this, I need to swim in the stars. I developed this technique in the desert on the playa."

She sat down on the green mossy plateau. She breathed in, thinking, *Abba, Abba, Abba*. She exhaled. *Shuaaaaaaa*. She then raised her legs straight up in the air, with her back flat on the ground. She looked up at the stars. She breathed in again. *Abba, Abba, Abba Shuaaaaaaaaaa*. She raised her arms straight up, aligned with her legs.

Then it was amazing. She started swimming. She started stroking slow, then fast, faster, furiously. She was entranced; she felt the vortex open in the Milky Way. She was sucked up into the atmosphere. She kept breathing. *Abba, Abba, Abba* (father). She exhaled. *Shuaaaaaa* (mother).

Then, as fast as she began, she stopped. She lowered her legs slowly, then her arms. Then came a big Abba Shua finish, and she lay still like she was in a coma. Then she popped up like toast. *"Eureka!* I have it!"

"I, Sissy Sprout, shall go to Smoke Fountain and ask this double-edged question: My majestic Mr. Smoke Fountain, wisest, coolest cat in the kingdom, please, O omnipotent one, tell me, a mere servant girl, how I might increase my tatas so as to fulfill an ancient prophecy and, in doing so, satisfy a king. The king. King Ahlowya. And then he will become enlightened, and I won't have to come back for the next question, which is, How do I obtain that glittery, shining object in the center of the pool of Clear Blue Easy? You see, my heart is set on obtaining that shiny object. I want it more than I've ever wanted anything. And a necessity has been laid on me by **Big Daddy** to breastfeed the King Ahlowya, but the king says my boobs are too small. So, Mr. Smoke Fountain, that is my question."

"Don't try to be slick, Ms. Sprout. He'd call you out in a New York second. It's either the boobs or the bauble. Make up your mind."

"Ah ha! I heard that King Ahlowya is really King Soloman and this cat, Smoke, you say, is his mouthpiece. Well, I figure if I breastfeed King Ahlowya and he *is* Smoke Fountain, then I will be in his favor. And he will have to use his wisdom to take me under. I mean underwater. Water under the bridge. Bridge over troubled water. Bridge over the River Quay. Anyway, he would owe me a favor for nourishing him, nurturing him, and healing him. So, Neo, what do you think?"

"I think it's absolutely gassy! Gassy, gassy, you rock, little sprout girl. That's an idea. When do you want to embark on this endeavor?"

"Right now, the time is now. We are here, need I say more? Oooohhhh, ooooohhh, I'm going to Smoke Fountain to make my boobs into mountains, to suckle the king. For me to get that glittering thing," she sang in a singsongy little sprout voice that made some noise.

So Sissy and Neo went gaily down the stream, as Neo couldn't travel out of water and he was the one who knew the way and had connections to see Smoke. So merrily they strolled, admiring flowers as they went along.

They turned down the creek, and it started getting real shady. The trees were real slim, slim and shady. It gave the appearance of a shadowy alignment that could take you off the beaten path (so to speak). The trees were old, and they had these knowls on them that looked like eyes.

In fact, as Sissy walked through the valley of shadowy trees, she feared no evil 'cause her staff was beside her. Her staff was called Pleasantness. It was a walking stick with a beautifully curved, contoured handle that all her fingers fit perfectly for balance.

Sissy always had a problem with balance. She had one leg shorter than the other and one arm shorter than the other. Her lips were uneven. Her nose was odd. She had a cowlick where her center part was supposed to be. She never was on center.

She strove to be on center. She knew of its importance. Time just flew out the window every time her inner being tried to lend a helping hand. For one thing, her curiosity led her mind to wander. When it wandered, it took so many directions—up, down, all around. Sometimes she was in a state of dizziness just from her wandering mind.

This quest—this immediate quest to fulfill a divine prophecy—was the most focused she had ever been for one purpose. Actually, she had turned it into a dual purpose. Remember, it started out with a quest to breastfeed the king. Next thing you know, she was intent on getting the glittery thing at the bottom of Clear Blue Easy.

Neo was getting along swimmingly with Sissy. He was a leader. Neo was at the head of his school of fishes. His gold was of the most iridescent class. His scales were perfectly, symmetrically aligned. His mouth was not too big, not too little. Neo's eyes were unlike any goldfish's eyes she had ever seen. They were blue, but not just any blue. She called them arctic blue.

Sissy called out, "Break time! I need to re-up my energy level." The sun was straight up, even with her vision. She took a deep breath and stuck her palm up, blocking the rays, with her body centered and her shoulders aligned.

She was in perfect symmetry. Awesome sunshine flooded into her body. Next, she stuck out her other palm. Then, because she only wore slippers, she stuck out the sole of her foot to suck the rays into her foot. She had too many rays in the past—Raymond, Ramon, and the bloody Ramones from the '70s. Now she partook of the sunrays only.

Ahhhhhhhh. The sunshine was healing, so she partook with gustatory gusto. **Big Daddy** was always horny; He infused His subjects with sexuality through His sunrays. Get it, rays? Moon rays, get it? Moon rays and star rays. Get it, star rays?

Oh my god. Literally, as she arched her back to meet each thrusting ray, she felt it on her C-spot, her O-spot, and after it entered, finally, her G-spot.

"Oh *solo mio*, don't say a word. Meaning *hush! Hush!* My darling, don't say a word. Mama's going to buy you a mockingbird. If that mockingbird won't sing, Mama's going to buy you a diamond ring. If that diamond ring turns brass, Mama's going to buy you a looking glass. If that looking glass gets broke, Mama's going to buy you a billy goat. If that billy goat won't pull, Mama's going to buy you a cart and bull. If that cart and bull turn over, Mama's going to buy you a dog named Rover. If that dog named Rover don't bark, Mama's going to buy you a horse and cart. If that horse and cart won't pull, Mama's going to buy you a cart and bull. If that cart and bull fall down, you will still be the sweetest little girl in town."

"Now that we all got our rocks off, it's time to go to work." Little Ms. Sunshine a.k.a. Sissy Sprout was way rejuvenated and restored to her same self, selfsame. "OK, Neo, duh, which way do we go?"

Neo said, "Darling Sissy, the direction you and I always take. Forward." And off they went.

Now we are getting down to the jungle, not to be confused with the forest. This was real green. Actually, it was unreal green. I don't think there were enough names for these shades of green. Some plants were oozing green goo. There was a phosphorescent glow over everything growing. It was utterly fascinating to behold.

This jungle of earthy delights had a tree in the center of the garden. There were two totem poles on either side, and the poles each had a head on them. The pole on the right side of the tree had a head that was strange. It was big and lumpy, with two of the largest, saddest eyes she'd ever beheld. In fact, she was drawn to them even though the head was frightening in a way she had never felt.

At first glance, the head, ugly as it was, was fascinating. The ugliness of it was more that it was so different (not human). It was an alien head, not belonging to this world. Odd. Now that she stared at it, she was drawn to it. She saw something in the eyes that no human had ever conveyed to her. It was healing. The face had the look of sadness, but not sadness for himself. It was a sadness directed at her.

It was as if you took all the compassion in the whole universe and put it into two pairs of eyes and then directed it straight at her. Yes, it was directed straight into her own two eyes.

As she accepted the glance, she became entranced, and a warm glow entered her being, like embryonic fluid. She realized that with the glance, look, stare of compassion, she was healed of every word or deed or action that had ever made her feel ashamed.

This totem pole head of an alien was sucking shame from her body, from her fingers, from her toes, from her nose, from her eyes, from her ears. Hell, the feelings of shame were sucked clean from her soul. That was some sucking done. The eyes of compassion did not miss one little bit of shame. Ooooohhhh, how good it felt to be sucked free from shame. There were no more voices in her head telling her what a bad girl she was.

She felt heavenly feelings of cleanness. She felt clean, finger-licking clean, inside and out.

Where was Neo as all this was going on? Neo was upright in the water, like a dolphin trained to dance. He was backpedaling his little tail, and his arctic-blue eyes were spinning round and round in his head like a hypnotist wheel, spinning, spinning.

Remember, he is a goldfish. Think of a goldfish with a goofy grin and his big red tongue hanging out to one side, to the left side. She had never seen a funnier sight in her whole life. She was freshly cleansed of every shameful word, act, and thought from her being. She was cracking up, busting a gut, belly laughing.

Neo couldn't speak. He couldn't stop. He was out of control. Then he caught Sissy out of the side of his head, and the sight of her hysterically laughing at him drove him over the top.

His spasm turned to humiliation. His embarrassment turned to anger. It made him dive headfirst into the River of Sighs. When they entered the jungle of earthly delights, the pool of Clear Blue Easy had entered the River of Sighs; so here was our golden boy.

The fish leader of the pack went down, down into the River of Sighs before Sissy could stop laughing. Wow! What a rush! She was too amped up to care about her newfound friend. She was sunny and bright, and all she wanted to do was dance.

Oh my god, she was dancing. Her feet were flying—kicking and stomping and jumping. She was clapping her hands, and her face was shining. Joy! Happiness! Freedom!

She exclaimed, "Hale luia, al le lu ia, hall le lu yah!" Whatever was the exclamation of ultimate guilt-free joy and energy and emergence, which were indescribably delicious.

For the first time, she didn't want to rush out to tell everyone else or pass it along or not believe that this feeling was solely for her, exclusively for her. It would never have the same effect if tried by another human or species of any kind.

In other words, it was joy that was right up her alley that had not been earned by any other human or otherwise, that she alone had the necessary ingredient to experience—the complex yet oh-so-simple key that was open and available to all mankind.

But it was deemed of so little value and was overlooked and ignored and sneered at, laughed at, mocked, and also used as a scapegoat for all of man's sufferings. Well, this misfit of a girl and eccentric young woman (wow man) had somehow, through all her hardheadedness to ever *dis*believe what she deemed **Big Daddy**'s unfailing word, and inability to lie, along with her diligently searching, as a pirate does for treasure, with complete faith regardless of reward.

Regardless of the laws of nature, regardless of reputation, regardless of imprisonment and torture, hatred by all humans and being alienated from society and family ties or normalcy, she obeyed the voice inside her head that never stopped guiding her, that never turned off or gave up.

It never abandoned her, no matter what state of mind she was in. It would patiently understand the way she thought and all the mistakes that made her thinking and reflexes so street, so ghetto, so gangster that she could never be a suburban white example, a cog in a well-oiled machine that gobbled up humans, resources, time, and energy without giving a thing back whatsoever. It was never satisfied, and it never let you relax. It started with a watch then went to the television, computer, cell phone, etc. Today is "throw your cell phone out the window" day. No talk in the 2000s.

We will leave that hot topic for another day. Meanwhile, the birds were singing, the stars were shining, and the clouds had linings. Sissy Sprout was trying to untie a bowrain. Oops. I mean rainbow. It was beautiful.

As hard as she tried, she couldn't untie the bow of rain a.k.a. rainbow. She climbed to the very peak and straddled the bowrain and slid all the way down, down, down, all the way to the ground. She landed—*splash*—right on her butt in the River of Sighs.

Now where was that goldfish? What was his name? Neon? Dayglow? No, that was wrong. No, no, no. Neanderthal? Yea, tha—. Hell no! He wasn't Neanderthal. He had looked like one, or what she imagined one looked like. But Neo, her golden boy with the arctic-blue eyes, had strangled a newborn idea and had quite discombobulated her.

Never defeated, she asked herself where the hell he was. *Sweet Jesus*. She missed his accent, the way he was so positive, and his street thinking. She missed his attention to detail and his calm amid all her ranting and raving. She went to the edge of the pool. She was midway between the river and the pool.

She felt like a bit of a fool 'cause she had just fixated her eyes. She was trying to focus. The more she tried to focus, the more her eyes would not focus. It got very boring trying to focus. She crossed her eyes. She stuck her tongue out. She jumped up, brushed herself off, and said, "Jolly whiskers, what if he never returns? Holy moly, no way!"

Well, she didn't want to think about that now. Not today. She'd think about that tomorrow.

***

Tomorrow came and went with no distraction. "***Big Daddy***," she called. "Have You no heart? I'm Your slave girl, but ***Dad***, what is this madness? I am utterly, completely alone. Am I to understand that this task to breastfeed the king is to be undertaken with no assistance, no guidance?" In other words, did she have to figure it out herself?

What an awesome concept. She was to tap into her own resources. She was to figure it out by acting like she was the only one on the planet and her figuring it out was necessary for the survival of the whole human race. Maybe she needed a minute to collect her thoughts.

What form of meditation should she employ? Maybe the upside-down planet would be the best achiever. It was worth a try.

She inhaled deeply. She centered herself and put her palms together. Then she bent from the waist, making her back flat. She bent down until she was looking backward between her legs. Then she locked her arms around her legs. She stretched and finished with a big Abba Shua.

She then faced east and did it again. This time, she put her elbows behind her knees and made a *w* with her fingers. This was very important. This *w* signified *watchtower*; that was code for *focus*.

She pointed the *w* up to her cho cha, her divine center of creation. Then she brought it down and swung it, pointed out, and at the same time, arched her back and gave a good stretch. She repeated this, bent from the waist backward, with knees locked, facing east, west, north, and south.

Aha! She decided to take the long way to Soloman's temple, and on the way, she would take nothing for granted. She would become a class

A observer, a classy observer. She would view her surroundings with the most intense gratitude and appreciation. She would view no moment as ordinary. Also, she would begin right now.

Let's see. She was at the foot of the mountain, and Smoke lived at the top. She could go straight up the beaten path. *Naaaah, that's too common.* She could start right here and spiral her way around the base, see everything the lower region had to offer then move up a notch and spiral again and again and again until she spiraled herself right up to old Smoke Fountain's front door. In the meantime, she would observe every flower, every bird, every creature that **Big Daddy** put on this planet. She would communicate on whatever level possible so she would become enlightened. She liked that idea.

The base of the mountain was rock, like a riverbed. Almost. There were huge granite-like rocks and slabs mixed with tufts of grassy wildflowers and poppies. There were red poppies and purple violets, with big yellow sunflowers. She didn't understand how these varied flowers could be so vibrant when they grew out of the rocks. She wished for an aerial view because she was certain there was a pattern, a method to the madness (so to speak).

All at once, a gigantic barn owl came and landed on a branch of a tree at the foot of the mountain. Did I tell you the name of the mountain? The local people called it Mount Shibboleth. But the foreigners called it Mount Sib due to the fact that they could not pronounce *Shibboleth.*

The tree was a mighty oak tree. It was very old and grew up about three stories high. The old owl was above her head, on one of the lower branches. "To whit to whoooo to whit to whooo," he called out.

She said, "Hello, Mr. Owl, what are you up to this fine evening?"

He said, "I spy with my little eye something on the ground that starts with *G.*"

"Oh, I know this one," Sissy Sprout said. "Oh my owl, is it a girl? Is it me?"

Mr. Owl said, "By Jove, I think you've got it! Quite smart for a girl your age, are you?"

"Yes, Mr. Owl, I guess I am. What do they call you?"

"They call me Owlllly. And what is your name, dear girl?"

"I am called Sissy. Sissy Sprout."

"Well, Sissy, you look like a lovely young lass. Where do you come from?"

"I come from a town called Madness, and I'm on my way to Soloman's temple to seek advice from Smoke Fountain, the coolest cat this side of Venus. Do you have any advice for a girl all alone in the world at this moment?"

"Hmmmm, you say you're going for advice from Smoke Fountain, and you want advice from me? Dear girl, maybe it would help if you told me what advice you'd like from the cat. Dear young lady."

"Oh yes, I must seem like an imbecile. Well, the advice I need from the cat is how to get that glitter thing in the bottom of the pool of Clear Blue Easy. And since I'm only allowed one question per lunar cycle, I was trying to combine my requests to get two for one. From you, I was going to ask, because you have an aerial view of this mountain, which is the best way to the top, to the temple? And how do these lovely flowers grow between these rocks? And is there some pattern? And where is their water source?"

At this, Owlllly perched on the branch closest to Sissy and was silent. His big blinking eyes were activated, and it looked like he was doing some thinking. Then he said, "Sissy, old girl, I'm going to reveal to you a sacred secret that has never been revealed up until now. You see, I will take you to the entrance, and then I will have to wait until you find the next exit to enter the next entrance and so on and so on and scooby dooby dooooo shaaaa shaaaa.

"This is a numerical, magical, labyrinthine mountain. You must enter at the base of the two snails' island. Two snails, Timmy and Bimmy, are eternal guards for the local people. Now I'm going to take you to the grassy knoll that is the spot where you will find the two snails. Have you ever seen snail trails, Sissy?"

"Nooo, I don't think that I have. What do they look like?"

"You will need a piece of glass to magnify. Get on your hands and knees and look for two slimy trails of no import. But to you, they have *big* import, as they will lead you to the entrance. Where the trails lead, you must follow, and when the two trails meet, you must stop. You must stop and look under the mat with the key. That is when you knock three times and insert the key.

"A door opens from the floor, and you will see twenty-four steps. These steps are tricky, and every fourth step is rotten. Every seventh step bounces, throwing you off balance. Every tenth step vibrates and heats up quickly. Every eleventh step returns to number one. So either trust your instincts or sit down and calculate what steps you must take. Then at the bottom of the twenty-four steps are twelve steps. They are programmed to trick you into thinking you have come somewhere important in your life when in reality, they can keep you from true progression.

"You see, these steps go backward. Yes, isn't that strange? So it's an illusion of progress. It's total regressing, regression. So avoid the twelve steps and look to your sharp right, and you will see an *L*. That is the elevator. What you do is push the button that says Later, and sooner than you know it, it will be later. You will have been transported. Rapid recovery to the center of the mountain. I suggest you get started. By the looks of the sky, you have three hours of daylight.

"So I say to you adieu to you, Ms. Sprout, it's been delightful. I will give you a few spins and point you in the right direction."

He spun her twelve times to the right and twelve times to the left. Then he said, "Count twenty-four steps forward. Pause! Reflect! Advance!"

She stopped. She centered, pressing the palms of her hands together in the center of her being, by her heart. She pushed her hands and arms, outstretched them, and expelled all negativity, feeling free and alive. She set forth on her journey.

As she walked around the bend, there was a boulder as big as a house. There was a waterfall falling gently on the rocks below. She advanced cautiously toward the big flat granite rock. It was there she beheld a sight no decent woman worth her salt would deny to be an utter revelation. Sunning himself on the rock was a chocolate glaze–covered armadillo. He was honey colored, and he had a chocolate-glaze covering that did not melt.

It was a hard shell, and it emanated the scent of chocolate. He was beautiful to behold. He was the color of honey and chocolate. The honey color was golden.

His eyes were small and golden. He was hanging out on the rock, totally unaware that he was being watched. She felt like being a voyeur. She waited and she watched. This was not just a chocolate armadillo. It was a honey-chocolate armadillo.

She was mesmerized. She stopped and hushed herself. She focused her gaze. She concentrated on slow, deep breathing and examined this creature. She took in the complexity of his surface, his outer shell. It was the deepest, richest brown. It looked liquid, but she couldn't be sure.

She thought to herself, *I must speak to him. I wonder how I should approach him. Should I sneak up on him, or should I stand still until he notices me? Hmmmm.* She observed a certain shyness about this creature.

She said to herself, "I'm going to walk out and pretend I haven't seen him, and if he speaks, then I will answer. If not, I will continue my journey as I do have a purpose and I am in no need of him or his companionship. I'll just strut myself before him and throw caution to the wind because he is a magnificent creature."

She centered her being. She stepped out gingerly and walked with grace. Immediately, he raised his head. He looked at her, and their eyes locked for a minute. His eyes widened with what looked like surprise mixed with delight. He said with a curious accent, Southern, slow, "My, my, my, what are you doing here?"

The friendliness in the way this was said opened her up to him. It drew her in. She held his gaze and said, "I am on a quest for **Big Daddy**. Part of this quest entails my going to the top of the Mount Sib to get an audience with Smoke Fountain and ask for his wise wisdom and advice on a personal question. So I just entered the entrance of the two snails, Timmy and Bimmy. By chance, I'm walking this way. Who are you?"

"Oh, excuse me, lil dahlin'," he drawled in a low, husky voice that had a soothing effect. "They call me Don-De-Tex, and that's my name. I'm a Texan chocolate-honey armadillo. My shell is very sought after. You see, it's like armor, only it tastes like liquid chocolate honey. Have you ever tasted that?"

Now Sissy had stopped listening and was imagining just how good chocolate honey would taste. Those were two of her favorite foods. This armadillo's eyes were the color of honey.

This armadillo was looking at her with a look that was almost familiar. Like maybe he thought she'd like a taste of that honey, chocolate honey. And guess what? She did!

She refrained. What a world, when a servant girl (human) could long to lick the back of a Texas armadillo. She had no shame. Plus, she was so tired. Her mama had always said, "Honey, if you feel like you can't go on and your hope is almost gone, reach out!" Reach out and partake of raw honey. She realized she was plotting.

She said to him, "Good day, Don-De-Tex. I am Sissy Sprout. I've been traveling the long and winding road. It looks like it has led to your door. I'm exhausted and a little gritty. I was listening to the waterfall, and I was contemplating getting a little dunk, a little cooling. I hope I'm not disturbing you. I'm dying to ask you. Have you ever had your shell licked by a human, boy or girl? Young or old? Whatever?"

"As a matter of fact, Ms. Sissy, I have. It was the winter of '72. I was a wee un. I was just knee high to a grasshopper, and this little girl came roller-skating down the sidewalk. She didn't see me. She tripped and ran smack into me. Flew over the top of me and landed in the rose bush. You see, it was really awful. Pretty little filly just a-singing and roller-skating happily down the walk, and then there's me, reading the newspaper.

"I saw her too late. I tried to ball up, but *slam*! She slammed me. I scooted across the walk and turned around, and the poor lil dahlin' was jammed in the yellow-rose bush, bleeding and a-crying in shock, afraid and desperate.

"I went to her and grabbed her little hand, and I said, 'Little dahlin', look into my eyes.' She stopped sobbing, and she looked up at me with these incredible green, gold, brown eyes that looked at me like I was the last Coke in the desert.

"I took out my machete. I cut through the brambles, and I extracted the little girl out of the bushes without harming the roses. That little girl was soooo grateful that she licked me from here to Arizona. Then she licked me back to Tallahassee. And she flipped me on my back and started on my underbelly, and finally, I had to beg her to stop cause this Texan had been licked out, licked out of my mind.

"And I was a little gruff with the girl. My voice is deep. I didn't explain to her that I did actually enjoy it, but I wasn't ready for all that licking. It took me off guard. So I scarred lil Donajean off. She just scampered. She was like a jumping spider. She was here one minute and gone the next, without a trace.

"I haven't seen her since, but I think of her often and wish I'd just let her lick her little heart out. She was just so grateful, and she had all this energy. She was into it very heavy. It was awesome. But bad timing, I suppose. So yes, Ms. Sissy, I have been licked by a human girl."

"My, my, my, that's some story, Don-De-Tex. I have to say that just seeing you does bring that out in us human girls. You see, chocolate and honey are things that girls value. We know that when we partake of them, first, we are going to get pleasure and a dopamine feeling in our brain. And then honey gives energy to the tired one. So you get pleasure and energy. Hey, Don-De-Tex, can I just have a taste of that hard outer shell?"

"Well, of course, Ms. Sissy. Come on over here and get you a little taste. They say it is sweetest right here by the tip of my tailbone."

"Oh, thank you, Don-De-Tex, that's what I want to know. OK, now hold still. I don't want to tickle you. (*lick, lick, lick*) My, my, my, my, this is delightful. (*lick, lick, lick*) Dee-lish-y-o-so! Wow! Is this addictive? Ummmmm. Ummmmmmm, Ummmmmm. Hold still, Don-De-Tex. Hey, quit squirming. Get back here, Don-De-Tex. OK, OK. I get it. It must be hard just to allow all that licking. I apologize. Here, I'll stop. Come here, let me look at you. Let me see if you are all right. How are you feeling, Don-De-Tex? You OK?"

"Yes, Sissy, I'm used to it. This sort of thing happens all the time. I'm a free spirit, and I'm friendly. Sometimes people read me the wrong way. But basically, I enjoy life, and I take chances. If things go wrong, I always have my shell."

"Oh, good, then I haven't harmed you. That's great. Well, I, ah, better be on my way. It was nice meeting you. Bye-bye."

And that was the beginning of a beautiful friendship. When she set her face to the east, where the sun was rising, she felt energy and pleasantness resonating in her being.

As she took off from the waterfall, she happened to look down at the ground. She saw something slimy, gooey, wet, and long on the ground. She took out her magnifying glass, and she got down on her knees and peered intently.

As she peered, a revelation was given to her that this was the trail of the two snails, Timmy and Bimmy. OK, now she was on to something. She would meticulously follow it and thus be on the path to the entrance. She was excited but relaxed.

She got down on her knees and crawled slowly so she wouldn't get off track. She saw that the world was sometimes a bit smaller than you or I know. There was definitely a lot of activity going on down there, on a lower level. She'd just never noticed.

She saw an organization of bugs, insects, aphids, moss, flora, and fauna. Dirt. Hell, even the dirt was different this low. How low can you go? Well, sometimes she'd see little mounds of something. It looked like dirt. But snails eat dirt. Was this regurgitated dirt? She suspected that it was. Then the trail stopped short.

Now where were those two, Timmy and Bimmy? How do you call a snail? Oh, your yoo-hoo wouldn't work. Maybe whistle? But at what frequency? Maybe a drumbeat?

Well, she decided to hum. She hummed a tune. First she hummed a hymn from her youth. That didn't work. She sat on a rock and waited. Nothing!

She decided to hum a love song, a famous one about loving and losing. It was a sad love song.

And out from a rock came one of the two snails.

This was the first time she had laid eyes on him. For one thing, for something so small, he gave the appearance of something quite big. It wasn't so much his size as it was his attitude. Kind of goo la ga ga te, you know. Kind of a smart aleck, cocky, a tad superior, and very interested and curious.

I'd like to take this time to introduce you to Timmy, the snail. He was not just any old snail; he was a psychedelic twin snail. He was off the scale as far as snails were concerned. Are we to believe the shell was hot pink and turquoise, the colors alternately spinning like a hypnotist wheel? His eyes were the same wheels, only one was fuchsia and the other was teal. His little antennae on his head were two purple dots on springy sticks. But let's talk noses. Snails were not supposed to have noses, but this one did. It was a noble honker.

He was not saying a word. He had the biggest smile, and he kept smiling until he was nose-to-nose with her. You see, she was lying on her stomach, crawling slowly toward the east. Timmy was going west. They met face-to-face.

She was staring a mite rudely. Well, maybe it was those crazy psychedelic eyeballs. In fact, she was sure that was it. One eyeball rotated ever so slowly to the right. His left eyeball rotated very fast to the left. Now you try looking at that eyeball-to-eyeball. She was dizzy in the head.

You know what? It was exhilarating! She was alive, and she liked the feeling. She thought about what she was feeling, and she came to one conclusion.

One thing. Pure energy. Pure natural energy. Now that was a switch.

Pure natural energy. She didn't want to waste a minute because she had a moment of clarity and realized this was her lucky day. This was the break she was waiting for.

She was with Timmy, the psychedelic twin snail who guarded the entrance to Mount Sib. Then she would be in like flint. Inside the labyrinthine mountain. This charming little snail was the one she had to follow closely. She could not let him get out of sight. Just because he was tiny didn't make it any easier. So she decided to stay on her belly and get squirmy. You can imagine. Think like a worm. Think like a worm?

The first step is to learn how to wiggle. Wiggling is an art. She'd been wiggling most of her life, wiggling out of sticky situations. Now she must wiggle her way into Mount Sib. First, the entrance.

She wiggled her way up to Timmy and looked him right in his antennae eyes and said in a low, husky voice, "Hi, big boy, why don't you come up and see me sometime?"

Timmy took one look at this big ol' girl lying on her belly, wiggling back and forth like a female worm, and he lost it. He fell head over tails in intoxicating, adoring, gotta-have-it love. His two spinning eyes just started spinning out of control. Blinking psychedelic lights were all over his body.

He was a beautiful baby! He was lit up like a Christmas tree. His face had the biggest smile, and he had the appearance of a snail that would go to extreme lengths to please her, the object of his attention and affection. She liked it. He was pretty to look at, and he was hysterically funny.

She was tempted to just park herself on a big ol' tree stump and watch his high antics, which were endless. He was standing on his tail end and trying so hard to reach up to her. He closed his eyes and puckered his lips. He rose tall and taller, and lo and behold. Be gosh and be glory. He was reaching up, up, up to meet her lips.

She was laughing and feeling as silly as a goose. She closed her eyes and puckered her lips and *smack*! He planted a kiss on her mouth.

As she kissed this psychedelic snail, something happened that was truly amazing. He didn't feel like a snail. The minute their lips met, she became unaware of her body and his body. There were only two pairs of lips coming together, touching and meeting and greeting in a manner that was as if they were engaged in a ballroom dance contest. They waltzed. They danced the rumba; they did the cha-cha. Then they did a polka, then a twist, then they went into the watusi and flowed into the funky four corners. They ended with a slow double bump and grind. Were her eyes deceiving her?

As they kissed, he grew. He kept growing until he was six feet tall. He grew a neck then a head. All from those two lips. By golly, he turned into a man. He opened his eyes, and they were turquoise. His hair was white.

He looked long and hard and said, "*Hi*, my name's Bimmy, and I'm a boy. You see, my mother ran off with a used bug car salesman back in the '50s. Her father lost it because he had introduced her to the man when he brought Mama in to pick out a new red Beetle for her birthday. Yes, and this used bug car salesman charmed my mama into running off to a small town in Arkansas.

"So, for revenge, her dad went to a hoodoo woman. He made a bargain with her to punish his daughter for not marrying Biff, the town hero who was going to give her father a black stallion. So he, in his anger, gave the Beetle to the hoodoo woman named Mavis in exchange for a curse.

"If the bug man violated Mama and impregnated her, she would give birth to a bug. Well, Mama must have been the fertile type. She conceived twins—fraternal twins. So we have Timmy the snail and me, Bimmy the boy. The separation process was too complex (we are conjoined in the brain). We share the same brain. We just come and go at will. You never know what will bring about the change. It's not dependent on any one thing. But say, why do we need to talk specifics? I'm here, and I'm a man. I just kissed you, you little monkey face. I'd like to continue in that framework if I could."

"Wait a minute. Let me get this straight. You were a snail, and now you are a man. But either way, you are the guardian of the entrance?"

"Yes, I am the guardian in whatever form I happen to be."

Sissy needed a moment to think. She had no use for a man. This smelled like a trap. She was going to exit stage left until she figured out how to deal with a snail. She had no time for a double-speaking, two-faced apparition that could change in an instant.

*Oh hell, **Big Daddy**! What the holy moly is this? Do You not want me to succeed? I'm feeling a little small about now, like maybe I bit off more than I can chew, like maybe I was overconfident or didn't calculate just how difficult this may be.*

What started out as an innocent act to breastfeed King Ahlowya turned to be . . . Damn it! It had been many moons since that day in the court of the king.

My, my, my, she really had some balls. The king had looked like he had been amused, and he wasn't mean. Maybe she could do this without Smoke Fountain's advice; maybe there was a different way to make her boobs bigger. Hmmmmmmm! She needed to meditate. She needed to really concentrate.

She started to hum. As she hummed, she danced in a circle. She moved herself and her energy around till she got her rhythm going. She went to the left for fifteen minutes, then she switched and went to the right for fifteen minutes. Then she decided she needed to do it some more.

She jumped up, and she said, "The price of this encounter is too high to pay. I will file this moment in my freeze-frame file. I'll return the opposite way I entered. If **Big Daddy** says to return, then I will return. If He doesn't, I will pretend that this was all a dream." That's what she always did when she had encounters that were not quite believable. She pretended she dreamed it. That way, when she spoke of it, she had no emotional attachment to it.

She was out and about, alone in a zone. She didn't even have a cell phone. Alone in a zone, she sat down on a flat rock about five miles farther into the mountain. She was walking away from a beautiful setting sun.

Guess what? She felt pretty darn good. Yet she was a little melancholic because that encounter had left her bewildered. She had kissed a snail that became a man who turned out to be a worm. What a world.

She felt the earth become squishy like thick moss, decadently spongy and so soft. She realized she was very tired.

She turned around and watched the sunset and sat on the ground. Then she curled into a fetal position, and before you knew what happened, Sissy was sound asleep before ten o'clock. She was not aware that she was being surrounded.

***

While Sissy snoozed, an army of ants were foraging for food from a discarded picnic basket. These ants were not the regular ones they had in her hometown. Theses ants were fire ants. Have you heard about them? They look small and helpless, but when they encounter flesh, its burning will send you through the roof. She bolted up. She scratched her leg. That made it worse.

She ran. She didn't have a clue where she was going. She ran! She huffed and puffed until she saw a babbling brook. She did not waste a second and plunged in. Oh yes, drown, you fire heathens from Hades!

Holy cow, what a way to wake up. She was flustered. She was hungry. She had to forage for food unless she ripped off the ants. She was focused.

She looked up at the heavens and said, "OK, **Big Daddy**, You got my attention. I realize I don't quite have the hang of this, as to what pertains to me and my purpose. And just what pertains. I've been blindly going forward, accepting this and accepting that." What she realized was that she had to get selective and maybe not so open or to stop expecting everyone to automatically be on board to aid her.

So she said, "From now on, I'll question if what I encounter is a healthy choice that has no wormwood effect and if it could be a direct gift from **Big Daddy**."

A little more effort and not so fast to make a decision, she invited **BD** (**Big Daddy**) to a powwow. It was a Gemini new moon. It was the first of June. There was a minor eclipse. This was the right time to humble herself and show what kind of servant she was—not one of lip service only, but one that could be delegated authority and that could accept responsibilities and bring honor and delight by her choices.

Now she felt radiant. She stuck her palms together in a warm handclasp, like the sealing of a covenant. She rose up. She felt taller than she ever had been. She felt a sense of approval.

It was as if the invisible realm of unseen forces were bearing her up on their shoulders and carrying her forward and cheering her on and proclaiming her victories. Enumerating them, she heard their version of her exploits. Apparently, she had done something right. Without her knowing or being aware of the importance, each of her choices had been on a far greater scale than she had ever imagined.

Her, Sissy Sprout! Little girl. The flat-chested middle child of human origins had made a whole invisible universe of souls, aliens, cherubs, and seraphim. **Big Daddy** Himself. They were applauding her unbelievable audacity to take her commission so seriously that she was excluded and written off as a megalomaniac nutcase, an overambitious psycho doomed to fail, even hoped to fail. Prayed to fail. Secret sabotage. Acting as if aiding but, in reality, wasting her precious time on false offers and nagging doubts and cruel contempt.

Now she shook them off. She shook her body like a dog out of water. Shake, girl! Shake them off! You must do what you must do. Is there no one genuine in the world? Are there no true believers? To be the only one in the whole planet Earth out of all humans? All women? It was incomprehensible! *How can I make this succeed?*

She was on the trails of the entrance. Must she find a way to get Timmy to lead her there? Was she smart enough? Did she even want to proceed? What was going to be her cost? What were the pitfalls? This was no cut-and-dried situation.

The most challenging feature was staying in the moment, not going too far into the future and not beating a dead horse about the past. She was here. She had made contact. She had come up with a flexible plan and a timetable for accomplishing it all.

It was February 2012. We would have two solar eclipses and two lunar eclipses; also, Venus would block the sun in December. The eclipses were in June and November.

By June, she needed to make contact with Smoke Fountain to ask about increasing her breast size to feed King Ahlowya and, ultimately, heal him.

She was overloaded. She had to go into dream state for all this to get sorted out through her subconscious. She would mindfully concentrate; she would find a grassy knoll (a fave of hers). She would wrap herself up in her snowflake tunic, close her little eyes, lay her little head down, and breathe in through her nose and breathe out softly through her nose. She would lucidly figure this quest out.

By tomorrow, she would wake up knowing exactly what to do. It was the Sabbath eve of Valentine's Day. Lover of all who loves. Where art thou?

"Did someone call for me?" She heard a voice that seemed older, sophisticated, charming, friendly, yet very confident that he was exactly who she was calling for.

Wow. "I have got to stop and partake of sacred budda so that my words may truly describe this." Hold on. (*inhale*) *Abba, Abba, Abba.* (*exhale*) *Shuaaaaaaaa.*

This budda really did slow her down so she could take in her surroundings, like trees. Now, after two hits, she was razzle-dazzled by the shade of purple of the tree that was covered in buds. The branches were like arms reaching out, and there were different shades of black, brown, and gray on the bark. Not to mention the knolls that looked like faces. What about the roots? old and winding into the earth.

Then she looked at the sky. She noticed how many shades there were of blue, purple, white, and gray. She noticed the shapes they made and how they changed with the drift of the wind.

You couldn't see the wind, only the effects of it. You could feel it so finely. She tuned in to nature. She smelled the sky; it smelled like sunshine and possible rain. She liked that smell.

Then she removed her sandals. The grass was abundant, so soft and green. She walked, and she stood and stretched until she was clearheaded, about as clearheaded as the rooster at dawn, ready to crow. She wanted to crow because, all of a sudden, she realized that for a small girl, she really had come quite a way on her own. She hadn't gotten in too much trouble. She had met some real characters.

Before she got too smug and self-satisfied, she took a loaf of bread from her bag and a little sample bottle of wine, which she got from her friend at the Mardi Gras café.

She took the bread and said a prayer of thanksgiving and forgiveness. She broke off a piece and broke it up into crumbs on the ground and said, "**Big Daddy**, bless the tiny creatures with this bread."

Then she opened the wine. She smelled the cork and gave thanks again, and she asked for forgiveness for all the crooked politicians and fat-cat religious leaders and greedy corporate businessmen. She sincerely wished they were not destined for obliteration.

She poured the wine on the ground after taking a sip and said, "**Big Daddy**, bless the vegetation. Let the wine give them joy to grow on. Let me treat the creatures and the vegetation as equal cohabitants of this world."

After that, a big rainbow appeared over the mountain. A door that she'd never seen opened up, and neon lights were blinking, twinkling. She heard a saxophone wailing, and there before her were spiral steps, wet, glistening, damp, with a drip that dripped to the bass beat.

Man, Al Hirt was dead. Gato Barbieri left the scene long ago. Wynton Marsalis was a myth. He'd never really been seen but was told of over and over again. This was sexy, sultry. It brought to mind that her body was ripe, that she had been a virgin for too many moons. She wished tonight was her wedding night. That's what the sax did to her.

She decided to go down, even though she knew not where it led. *Here we go.* She centered herself. She breathed in deeply. What is that smell? Ummmmm, it was nice, fresh. It wafted up to her. It was so pleasant that it beckoned her to descend.

She trip-trapped down, creating her own rhythm as she went. As she descended, she began to see splashes of color. Splashes of color!

There were splashes of purple, splashes of white, splashes of yellow and purple. What were these splashes of color? All at once, singing broke out. It was a catchy tune. "Tell me who, who wrote the book of love."

Were the splashes singing? She had to get a closer look. They were kind of out on a ledge. She wasn't that tall, but she could climb. She stopped, and she scaled up two or three rocks.

Oh my, my, my, never in the real world. They were not aware of her. But they were very "aware." She got down from the rocks. She wondered if there were more singing morning glories. She decided to keep descending.

At the next ledge, she climbed three or four rocks. Yes! There were more singing morning glories. Only, these were singing "When the Saints Go Marching In." It was very uplifting. Really! Inspiring! Then she noticed the seeds. There were seeds everywhere.

It had been eons since she had any food. She wondered, if she ate some of these seeds, would she start singing a tune?

So Ms. Sissy Sprout climbed up onto a nice plateau, and she took seven morning glory seeds and put them in the palm of her hand. She pulled out her looking glass, and she thought to herself, *They look harmless.*

She fingered them individually. She licked them one by one. She sucked each seed for one hour and then swallowed it whole and went on to the next one. She sucked on it for one hour, then swallowed it. This went on till all she had left was an empty hand.

Then she raised her eyes to the sky. She said, **Big Daddy**, yoooooo hoooo, tell me what to doooo.

All of a sudden, a purple haze covered the plateau, and things took on a glittery edge. It was very pretty and happy. She was infused with a sense of well-being to a higher degree than before. Something instinctively told her to hush. Super-relax unwind. A voice was about to speak.

She saw a bush. There were flames coming from the bush, and inside she beheld tongues of fire. But the bush was not burning. It just had a reddish-orange glow, with a tad of blue and white. It was very beautiful and curious to behold.

Then came the voice. It was definitely **Big Daddy**. The voice was a cross between Jack White and Harry Connick Jr. It was very sexy and friendly, but authoritarian. It was incredibly appealing and entrancing.

"Remove your sandals, Sissy Sprout, for you are on holy ground."

At that, Sissy dropped to her knees and prostrated herself and then removed her sandals. She breathed in deeply, never taking her eyes off the bush. She couldn't understand fire that wasn't hot, fire that did not burn, fire with no singeing or scorching.

What kind of freaky deaky fire did **Big Daddy** possess? Well, she was extremely close to it. It gave no warmth. It was a visual fire. It had incredible movement. It was dancing, gyrating. It was not a slow, steady flame.

They were independent of each other. Many flames, same fire. All is one. Yeah! She couldn't do a thing but stare and wait to be invited to rise.

After a respectful moment of reverence, His voice beckoned, "Arise, my daughter. My faithful slave girl. My highly favored one. It is time I throw you a bone.

"You are one determined, unanswerable, unswerving human. You don't fall for tricks. You don't dillydally. You keep a smile and your openness.

"You seem very confident. Only I know you are much more interested in the shiny thing in the pool of Clear Blue Easy than you are about breastfeeding the king. I'm well aware of that fact. That is the reason that I am going to cut you some slack.

"You see, you have surpassed me and my cronies' original plan for who and how this was to be accomplished. You got right to it. You got results. So myself and my yes-men all agreed to grant you the glittering thing. I will tell you what it is. It is lungs for you—aqualungs. From this day forward, you will become aquatic, with land creature status, and then you will obtain the glittering thing, my daughter.

"At this moment, as we speak, your fingers are becoming slightly webbed from the finger to pinkie and slightly cupped for swimming efficiency. Your toes will be webbed, and you are growing gills at this very moment.

"Stand still and receive your new, improved multidimensional body. Stand erect and feel the magnificence of it all. You see, you deserve your reward ever so much. I'll tell you I'm not too pleased with King Ahlowya. He is vain, lazy, and pompous. He rejected my slave girl, my woman, the jewel that I've set aside as my own bride of eternity. And unlike King Ahlowya, I am willing to submit to you as my superfine goddess of ecstatic achievement.

"From this day forward, you are not destined for human love with any creature from the land, sea, or sky.

"You are to be my sole delight, my personal treasure. I will leave these earthlings to their new world order. I will rid the planet of the vermin. I will give them another instruction manual. We will fly the coop with you by my side, traversing the galaxies one by one at our leisure, cocreating beauty and awesomeness wherever the wind blows us. The Euroaquilo is on its way. My precious, beloved immortal, why don't you go to the pool of Clear Blue Easy, try your new aqualungs, and get that bauble while I get ready for showtime?

"I told them and told them. I sent my eldest son. I sent my prophets. I sent signs. I sent warnings. I sent curses. I sent pestilence, famine, war, insects, wild beasts, and floods. This time, I got something new for them."

"May I ask what it is?"

"Yes, my dove. Sit down, my sprout, visualize this: All earthquakes happen, and all volcanoes erupt at once. While fire shoots from the sky, showering ash and hot lava all over the planet, and the ground cracks and splits the USA into three separate pieces, I send hail from the storehouses. Giant hailstones. Fire and ice, oh so very nice. You were wondering about the bush. You see, when two different flames from two different fires burn together, the hotness of the one cancels the hotness of the other, making them quite cold, like dry ice. Imagine.

"Next, all zoos are opened wide. All beasts are free and seeking revenge on humankind. All insects converge. Eat! Eat! Eat! Nothing is left alive. There is severe famine.

"Then unsanitary conditions bring back the plagues of old—leprosy, tuberculosis, polio, the Black Death! Man, I tried to warn them! I really did! I was ready to forgive at the drop of a hat. But noooooo. They did not want it. They felt no regrets, no shame, no pity, no remorse, no self-conscientiousness.

"So what choice did I have left? I ask you. It is my universe. They became tenants who were the biggest niggers of existence. We are not talking of race or skin color. We are talking of behavior. The richest ones were the biggest niggers. Skinflints, tightwads, low-class, ill-mannered, deviants, immoral ignoramuses. Quite frankly, Sissy, I don't give a damn.

"So go ahead, Sissy, my love, you enjoy. Then go to the labyrinth and wait for the signal. Make the chain: humans, front-to-back links. Dance for twelve hours in one direction, then twelve hours in the other direction, and wait for the mountain to open to take you in for survival. Keep the chain renewed.

"Rest, trip, get stoned, hydrate, eat, fuck, enjoy. This won't take long.

"One-third survive."

THE END

Printed in the United States
By Bookmasters